Nineteenth Century America

THE
SPORTS

JOHN L. SULLIVAN

Nineteenth Century America

THE
SPORTS

written and illustrated by
LEONARD EVERETT FISHER

Holiday House · New York

Library of Congress Cataloging in Publication Data

Fisher, Leonard Everett.
   The sports.

   (Nineteenth century America)
   Includes index.
   SUMMARY: Discusses the development of athletic
competition in 19th-century America.
   1. Sports—United States—History—19th century—
Juvenile literature. [1. Sports—History]   I. Title.
II. Series.
GV583.F57   796'.0973   80-16467
ISBN 0-8234-0419-6

List of Illustrations

EARLY COLLEGE FOOTBALL

Author's Note

This book deals with the spirit and development of athletic competition in 19th century America. Physical skill, strength, and stamina were the preferable qualities sought in the games Americans played, but they were not always required. In other words, I have included football rather than checkers; rowing, not steamboat racing; roller hockey, not roller skating; and golf instead of marble shooting.

Competitive athletic activities—as opposed to physical exercises—played according to rules have been included. Noncompetitive pastimes and recreations have been excluded. Thus ice skating around a frozen pond for personal pleasure is *out*.

So-called "sporting events" involving competitive animals, such as dog racing, have been excluded. The only exceptions are horse racing and polo. Bloody amusements like cock-fighting, bearbaiting, gander-pulling, ratting, buffalo-killing, turkey-shooting, and similar pastimes involving animals are *out*. Some forms of man's inhumanity to man are *in*: eye-gouging, choking, bone-breaking wrestling matches, for example; and bare-knuckle fighting.

Draw and stud poker, favorite variations of a card game popular with the coast-to-coast "sporting crowd," from mining camps and Mississippi River sidewheelers, to saloons and eastern private clubs, are *out*. So's courtin' and frog-jumpin'.

"P-L-A-Y B-A-L-L!"

THE ELYSIAN FIELDS, HOBOKEN, NEW JERSEY

ACCORDING to the ancient Greeks, the Elysian Fields were beyond this world, a glorious place where deserving heroes, selected by the gods, could live through all eternity. In the classical Greek mind, athletic heroes, like military heroes and others, never died. The ancient hero so rewarded went from this world to Elysium—to the Elysian Fields—where life continued out of the vulgar sight of ordinary mortals, in joyous and perfect surroundings, forever. Every Greek aspired to such a wondrous reward. It was the ultimate prize.

Many Americans, caught up in the blissful pursuit of life, liberty, and happiness at the onset of the 19th century, viewed their entire country as Elysium, as Paradise. They had already won the ultimate prize and were about to build a nation in the place.

Thomas Jefferson himself had fired the imagination for things Greek. He saw the American political system as being the heir of 5th century B.C. Greek democracy. Moreover, he encouraged the idea that new government buildings in Washington, D.C., the nation's new capital, reflect the Greek lineage of American politics and culture in their architectural splendor.

As far as the amateur Knickerbocker Ball Club of New York was concerned, the Elysian Fields in 1845 were definitely not in another world; nor could they be confused with the territory and promise of the United States. They were in this world—in Hoboken, New Jersey—a dreamy, romantic, but very real flat and grassy meadow surrounded by lush picnic groves and a cluster of thirst-quenching taverns. All this across the Hudson River from Manhattan.

A private park, the Elysian Fields was owned by inventor John Stevens, who helped introduce steam locomotives and railroads, among other things, to America. There, in the unspoiled, scenic New Jersey countryside of 1845, Alexander Cartwright and friends —28 fun-loving cronies with steady jobs and leisure time who socialized as the Knickerbocker Ball Club of New York—indulged their ball-playing passion in peace, far from the rush of New York City civilization which had now reached as far north as 27th Street.

And there, on the Elysian Fields of Hoboken, in sight of strolling lovers brought to the picturesque spot by

John Stevens' ferryboats, the Knickerbockers continued what they had started doing three years earlier on another meadow in Lower Manhattan, since buried under advancing civilization.

They, not Abner Doubleday, forged the rules of modern baseball and played the game—give or take a few refinements—much as it is played today. The Knickerbockers revised and made more adult and energetic a schoolboy game called town ball, or rounders, its British counterpart. Western Plains Indians beyond the Mississippi River still played a comparatively crude bat and ball game that was not too far removed from the idea of baseball. There, a batter stood in a circle and swatted a stuffed rawhide ball at any number of fielders. The fielder who caught the ball on the fly had the privilege of throwing it at the batter. If he managed to hit the batter, the batter was knocked out of the circle and became a fielder. The thrower became the batter.

In any case, town ball, or rounders, sometimes called baseball, and often called one o' cat, two o'cat, three o' cat, and four o' cat, depending on the number of bases used, had been played in Boston, Philadelphia, and New York in a variety of haphazard ways since before 1800. Gaining some momentum after the War of 1812, during which time English sailors impressed American seamen and English soldiers burned down the White House, American baseball gradually replaced the very popular British cricket, a game introduced to the colonies by the English about 1750.

Cricket incorporated rules and equipment seemingly similar to those in town ball, making it a distant ancestral cousin to the game of baseball being developed in the United States. The fact is, however, that cricket faded rapidly after 1820, not so much because most Americans did not think too highly of anything British after the war, but because cricket was not suitable to the American temperament. It was too slow, too courteous and genteel. Americans were more interested in speed, arguments, and excitement. Many a skillful American cricketeer became a baseball player by midcentury.

Alexander Cartwright was not only the manager, umpire, player, organizer, and chief inventive spirit of the Knickerbocker Base Ball Club of New York, he was also a gentleman surveyor. In 1845, he decided that bases had to be 90 feet apart in a perfect square and that

ALEXANDER CARTWRIGHT SURVEYING

the pitcher's position must be fixed exactly 60 feet from "home." There, at home, or "home base," the batters had stood for years ready to "knock the stuffing" out of stuffed leather balls.

The Knickerbockers changed several other practices. No longer would players run clockwise around the bases. Now they would run counterclockwise around the "diamond." And no longer could a fielder put a batter "out" by "plugging" or hitting him with the ball as he ran around the bases. The Knickerbockers continued to play as many innings as was necessary to roll up the required scores of either 11 or 21 runs. The team that scored 21 or more, or 11 or more, runs in an inning, and whose total score was more than that of the opposition, won the ball game. The Knickerbockers came to their games in uniform—blue floppy pants, white shirts, and straw hats—revolutionizing the look of the game.

On September 23, 1845, the Knicks drew up a set of bylaws and organized themselves into the first formal baseball team in America, and introduced the first fixed schedule of games. In addition, they invented the game book to record in detail every game played, the first of these being on October 6, 1845. As in the past, they played themselves. Cartwright's side lost. The score was 11-8 in three innings.

On June 19, 1846, the Knickerbockers did another remarkable thing. They played another team, the New Yorks. It was the first match game in baseball history.

The Knicks lost 23-1, playing according to the rules they themselves had devised and developed. There was much swearing, umpire-baiting—Cartwright was the umpire—and arguing. The game was beginning to lose its good breeding. Two other notable firsts concocted by the Knicks were the system of nine-player teams with substitutes called "muffins," and the fining of ball players for sundry infractions, including swearing.

By 1858, there were at least two dozen baseball clubs in the New York City area—the Gothams, Brooklyn Eagles, Brooklyn Eckfords, Jamaica Atlantics, Long Island Pastimes, Manahattans, and more. The players on these clubs, chiefly policemen, bartenders, mechanics, laborers, and assorted toughs, met in convention to

THE KNICKERBOCKERS VS. THE NEW YORKS

simplify and standardize the rules which varied from place to place. After much wrangling, they adopted the rules used by the Knickerbockers, who continued to lose more games than they won. They disappeared from the scene some ten or eleven years later, having done their work—establishing the modern game of baseball.

All during the Civil War (1861-1865), nearly every rest from the carnage of battle resulted in a baseball game. The mania was everywhere among Union troops. These Northerners brought the game south with them when they were carted off as prisoners-of-war. They introduced the game to their guards and wardens in the prison camps. By the time the war had ended, baseball had spread all over America. By 1870, the game had become professional. The Cincinnati Red Stockings, managed by an ex-cricketeer, centerfielder Harry Wright, were paid to beat everyone else. Only one of their hired players was from Cincinnati, first baseman Charles Gould.

In 1876, America celebrated 100 years of independence; Wild Bill Hickok, a federal marshal, was shot in the back in South Dakota; General George Armstrong Custer and his troopers died at the hands of Chief Sitting Bull and his warriors at the Battle of the Little Big Horn in Montana; Democrat Samuel J. Tilden received the most votes for President of the United States but lost the election to Rutherford B. Hayes; and the baseball pros founded the National League in New York. Five years before, however, on St. Patrick's Day, 1871, nine teams had formed the National Association of Professional Baseball Players—the first playing league. Those paying the $10 membership fee that day were the Boston Red Stockings, Chicago White Stockings, Cleveland Forest Citys, Fort Wayne Kekiongas,

New York Mutuals, Philadelphia Athletics, Rockford Forest Citys, Washington Nationals, and the Washington Olympics.

Riddled with crime and corruption, the league did not last four years. It was replaced by the National League with Hartford, Connecticut, businessman Morgan G. Bulkeley as its first president, and organized baseball became a more tightly supervised sport. Tickets cost about fifty cents a game. Modern baseball, a generation old in 1876—the game itself in all its recognized forms had been played for at least a half century—was beginning to live up to the promise and prophecy of one midcentury, forgotten author: "This game . . . bids fair to become our national pastime. . . ."

Without doubt baseball had quickly become a national craze among the American male population. The game certainly involved the largest number of participants— organized and unorganized, amateur and professional, boys and men. The game or sport of baseball became a distinctive and unique American institution, whatever its origins, before the 19th century had run its course.

Nonetheless, there were other sports, much older sports, which enjoyed a different American vigor and attracted far greater crowds in a single day than any baseball game ever did—then or now. One of these was horseracing.

Although the racing of thoroughbred horses—horses

bred only by crossing English and Arabian stock—did not become established and popular until after the Civil War, horseracing itself was an established fact in the British-American colonies not long after the Dutch gave up their New Amsterdam holdings to the British in 1664.

For the most part, horseracing in America was the "sport of kings." Only the wealthy bred and raced horses according to established rules. And only the wealthy built race tracks. One of the earliest of these was established at present-day Hempstead, Long Island, New York, during the second half of the 17th century. And only the wealthy offered each other prizes.

ECLIPSE VS. SIR HENRY

Back-country horseracing sponsored by dirt farmers, tradesmen, and tavern owners were usually disorganized, spur-of-the-moment activities involving few rules and fewer prizes, but brisk betting.

In the spring of 1823, however, American horseracing took on a different look. Virginian Colonel William Ranson Johnson was convinced that no Northern horse could ever beat a Southern horse. His Sir Henry was unbeatable. The challenge was made. New Yorker Cornelius Van Ranst, owner of American Eclipse, took up the challenge. So did nearly 100,000 heavy-betting, heavy-drinking Northerners and Southerners who jammed Union Course Race Track on Long Island.

The owners put up a purse of $20,000 for the horse who would win at least two of three heats on the mile-long course. The race was run on May 27, 1823. What seemed to be at stake was not only horseflesh but the honor of which section of the soon-to-be-divided country would prevail, North or South. The entire nation was interested in the outcome. The match was the first national contest between regional horses. In the end, the eight-year-old American Eclipse took not only two of the required three heats from his 4-year-old Southern rival, but also the money and the prestige. The honor of the North was saved. The South was humiliated.

It took twenty-two years for the South to even the score. On May 13, 1845, at the same track and for the same $20,000, a Southern horse named Peytona beat a Northern horse called Fashion.

The Civil War disrupted horseracing in the South. Because so many horses ended up in the Confederate cavalry, racing in the South came to a virtual halt; however, in the North it continued to flourish. Tracks abounded from New York's Saratoga Springs, which opened August 3, 1863, to Chicago and Cincinnati. Not long after the war had ended, more tracks emerged around the country, including the restoration of tracks in the deep South. Brooklyn, New York, boasted two well-attended tracks—Brighton Race Track near present-day Coney Island, and Gravesend Race Track at the junction of what is now Ocean Parkway and Kings Highway.

Most of these tracks, if not all of them, were oval in design. Oval tracks had been flourishing in America since the end of the 18th century, and since that time grandstands accommodating at least 10,000 people stood at the finish lines of major tracks.

A RACE TRACK GRANDSTAND

Three of the most famous American races were hardly noticed during the post-Civil-War period. All three were for three-year-old horses and have since come to be known as the Triple Crown of racing. The first of these is the Belmont Stakes, inaugurated at Elmont, New York, in 1867. The second is the Preakness Stakes, first run at the Pimlico track, Baltimore, Maryland, 1873; the third "jewel" in the Triple Crown began on Monday, May 17, 1875, at Churchill Downs, Louisville, Kentucky. Founded by M. Lewis Clark as the Kentucky Derby, the race has since been run yearly on the first Saturday in May.

While fast horses became more famous than their owners, the jockeys who rode them had their day in the sun, too. There was "Snapper" Garrison, who always seemed to finish first after being last most of the race. A contemporary of Garrison's during the 1880's and 1890's was Tod Sloan. Both Garrison and Sloan changed the technique of riding, thereby increasing a horse's speed. Instead of riding straight up in the saddle with their legs extended vertically—the traditional technique—these two jockeys shortened the stirrup straps, which bent their legs and forced them to ride higher in the saddle but crouching low and forward over the horse's neck. The position reduced wind resistance. It was called the "monkey's crouch," and was adopted by jockeys everywhere.

By far the most famous of all jockeys during the latter part of the century was Isaac Murphy, a black man. Murphy was the first jockey to bring home three winners in the Kentucky Derby—in 1884, 1890, and 1891. Also, he was the first jockey to produce two winners in two consecutive Derby years. These records stood for nearly half a century. He died in 1896, a wealthy horse owner and an American hero.

Harness racing, or trotting, a form of horseracing in which the "driver" sits in a two-wheeled sulky pulled by a horse that trots rather than runs, was perhaps the most popular and thriving of all sports during the 19th century, chiefly in rural America. There was hardly an American alive who, by the end of the century, had never heard of driver Hiram Woodruff, whose 30-year career ended in 1865; and Hambletonian, a magnificent horse who earned a fortune for a poor farmer.

A TROTTER

Harness racing in America actually began with the arrival in 1788 of Messenger, an English thoroughbred stallion. Messenger's sole mission was to sire running horses for American tracks. But instead of fathering sons and daughters that could run, Messenger sired offspring that could trot with a perfect gait. It remained for Messenger's great grandson, Hambletonian, to become the most prized trotter and sire of all. Hambletonian was born in 1849 and purchased by an upstate New York farmer, Wilhelm Rysdyck, for $125. Hambletonian was so handsome an animal, and so fast, that Rysdyck soon refused to race him. Instead, he preferred to use Hamble-tonian as a stud horse. By the time Hambletonian died in 1876 and was buried under a granite monument, he not only was the most famous animal in America, but he had sired 1,331 other magnificent trotters and earned nearly a quarter of a million dollars for farmer Rysdyck. Today, practically every trotting horse racing is descended from Hambletonian and thus can trace a lineage all the way back to Messenger.

One other major sport involving horses (other than New England log-pulling competitions, usually won by a breed called Morgans or Justin Morgans) was polo. Polo was known by few in America, but it was played during the last quarter of the century. The game was probably about 4,000 or more years old, having origi-nated in the Near East. The British discovered it in India and brought it to London in 1869. An American newspaper publisher, James Gordon Bennett—the very same Bennett who owned the New York *Herald* and the New York *Evening Telegram,* and who sent reporter Henry M. Stanley into the African jungles to find lost missionary David Livingstone—introduced the game to a few Americans in 1875.

POLO

The mallets and balls were imported from England. The small horses came from Texas, the idea being that a team of four men on horseback should use the mallets to drive the balls through the opponents' goal post. Bennett and some friends rented Dickel's Riding Academy in Manhattan in 1876 and played the first game of polo in America—indoors. The sport was played outdoors in Great Britain and elsewhere. This fast, spirited, often dangerous game was played indoors over the next four or five years before it went outdoors. The spectators were plentiful, and for the most part consisted of the upper strata of society. In 1886, Newport, Rhode Island, became the scene of the first international polo match to be held in America. The English beat the less experienced Americans two games to none.

Among the gentler sports were croquet, tennis, and golf.

Croquet was not too taxing a sport, or game, and was played all over the world, mostly in France where it was invented, in England where it was known as pall-mall, and in the early American colonies. The players, men and women—it was the first sport in America enjoyed by both men and women—simply tried to stroke a ball gently with a mallet through a series of wickets and arrive first at a goal post. Long considered a social pastime, its only requirement other than mallets, balls, wickets, and posts, was a flat grassy plot of ground, usually someone's front or back yard.

In 1864, some of the more sociable croquet players in Brooklyn organized themselves into the Park Place Croquet Club. The twenty-five-member club seeded other clubs around the city. Soon the game became popular enough to standardize the rules for inter-club competition. Accordingly, in 1882, the National Croquet Association was organized. From then on the intensity of the sport increased beyond the original croquet and a new game was born called roque. Roque was a faster game that few croquet-playing ladies had anything to do with. Wickets were still in use, and so were the end posts, mallets, and balls. The scoring was slightly different. But what made the big difference was the use of a low wall to surround a more compact, smaller course. The wall acted as a rebounding surface against which balls smashed at great speeds, caroming to destroy the positions of other balls and sometimes players.

CROQUET

Tennis and golf emerged on the American scene almost at the same time. Tennis was not altogether a new game when it was played on an outdoor American lawn for the first time in 1874. An indoor game called court tennis, requiring a racket to hit a ball back and forth over a net stretched across the width of a room, had been played for hundreds of years, and was still being played by the royal families of Europe and their households. In 1873, British Army Major Walter C. Wingfield, took the game of court tennis from indoors to outdoors, demonstrating it in Wales. Two years later, the English Marylebone Cricket Club drew up a set of rules and called the game lawn tennis.

TENNIS

Lawn tennis was brought to the United States in 1874 by an American traveler, Mary E. Outerbridge, of Staten Island, New York, where she set up a court. It was not long before the wealthy began laying out courts wherever they congregated. In England, within three years, the first of the great tennis tournaments was inaugurated at Wimbledon. Staten Island hosted a tennis tournament in 1880. A year later, the United States Lawn Tennis Association was chartered and America's second major tournament got under way at Newport, Rhode Island. "Dicky" Sears won the tournament and became America's first recognized tennis champion. He remained champion until 1889.

Sears proved that tennis was not necessarily a ladies' game, an image brought on by its running rhythms, its gentility, and its connection with Mary E. Outerbridge. Although American tennis was the sport of women at the outset, it soon changed direction when men realized the skill and stamina required for perfection. Tennis remained a sport in which both men and women participated. It was played primarily by the wealthy until well into the 20th century.

Golf entered the United States via the Canadian Royal Montreal Golf Club, which was established in 1873. The game was already a few centuries old, having begun in the British Isles, probably Scotland. In 1887, a golf club was organized in Foxburg, Pennsylvania. A year later, in 1888, the St. Andrews Golf Club was founded in Yonkers, New York, by two transplanted Scotsmen, John Reid and Robert Lockhardt. These two wheedled 30 acres rent free from a local tradesman and constructed a six-hole course for their club. They continued to play six-hole golf until 1894, when they moved their sport and club to another pasture, where they constructed a nine-hole course. There they set up a dress code for golfers—knickers, plaid socks, winged collars, caps, and jackets—a code that would persist on the "links" (a Scottish word for gently rolling land) for at least the next thirty or forty years.

Also, in 1894, the men of the St. Andrews Club—golf at this point was strictly for men—helped to organize the United States Golf Association and the championship tournament that was held that year in Newport, Rhode Island. The following year, 1895, the United States Golf Association sponsored its first national championship tournament at Newport. By this time, the Chicago Golf Club, located in Wheaton, Illinois, had an 18-hole course, the first in America, which had been constructed in 1893.

GOLF

Before the century would end, in 1896, women would be playing nine-hole golf for the first time at the course of the newly incorporated Shinnecock Hills Club at Southampton, Long Island. The club had opened in 1892 with seventy members who had paid $100 each for the privilege. Also in 1896, the City of New York opened the first public golf course at Van Cortlandt Park in the Bronx. There, for small fees, the public could play golf without having to belong to an expensive club. Thus encouraged, the general public responded and broadened the participation base of the game, making golf a sport enthusiastically pursued by tens of thousands of Americans from all walks of life.

Gymnastics and archery, along with target and trap-shooting, had their followers, too, in young 19th century America.

Interest in archery and gymnastics occurred about the same time and for the same reasons—health and recreation.

Physical fitness was an obsession of gymnastic enthusiasts as early as 1825. For them competition was not as important as posture and general all around robustness among men and women alike, although far fewer women than men involved themselves in gymnastics. Charles Beck, a German immigrant, opened a gymnasium in Northampton, Massachusetts, in 1825, and immediately attracted crowds of people interested in

GYMNASTICS

improving their physiques.

Beck offered regimens of exercise aimed at physical self-improvement. He also provided the equipment appropriate for exercising. There were flying rings and trapezes, parallel bars and "horses," chinning bars, and climbing ropes and ladders. Fencing was practiced with great spirit, although it took more than sixty years for it to surface as a sport with the founding in 1891 of the Amateur Fencers League of America. Beck also taught boxing—not as a sport, since it was illegal in most parts of the country—but as the manly art of self-defense.

Archery, the method of shooting with bow and arrow, is as old as prehistoric man. Though early man had little use for the bow and arrow as a sport, archery competitions were held from time to time throughout history. Nevertheless, from that dim beginning thousands of years ago to about the middle of the fifteenth century, the bow and arrow were used chiefly for killing people and animals. Gradually rifles replaced bows and arrows in the arsenal of mankind, and the bow and arrow were reduced mostly to shooting harmless targets.

Archery, the sport, was a royal recreation during the reign of English King Charles II, toward the end of the 17th century; and like many things British, it found its way to America. In the American wilderness, the white man found the Indian already a deadly marksman with bow and arrow. Soon, these too were replaced by rifles. The sport remained a disorganized amusement

34

until 1828. In that year, a group of young Philadelphia archers joined together to form The United Bowmen of Philadelphia, sporting a blue-and-white uniform. The club lasted through some thirty years of competition and prizes. But the sport enjoyed such popularity that in 1879 another club was organized, The National Association of Archers, which would one day become the National Archery Association.

Shooting a target with a rifle or revolver had always been an enthusiastic pastime among Americans everywhere and, like archery, it enjoyed a disorganized following with rules for competition usually made up on the spot. It was not until 1871 that rules for rifle matches or any manner of firearm competition were standardized by the National Rifle Association, which was formed for that purpose.

For the next quarter of a century, the National Rifle Association fielded teams of expert riflemen who competed for prize money and silver cups. In 1874, a National Rifle Association team shot against a championship team from Ireland. The match was the first international rifle competition held in America. The Americans won and went on to beat Ireland, Canada, Australia, Scotland, and England herself, in the years ahead. The Americans did most of their winning on a rifle range in Creedmoor, Long Island, New York.

Trapshooting, a sport in which a clay-like target, or "pigeon", is sprung from a trap and the shooter has to hit it in flight with a shotgun from a distance of about 25 yards, was just getting underway as the 19th century ended. The American Trapshooting Association was founded in 1900 to establish rules for the sport. "Skeet" shooting was a later development of trapshooting. Here the shooter had to hit the flying target from an assortment of angles.

Many 19th century Americans owned rifles or other firearms, usually for sporting and hunting reasons, but often for self-defense in hazardous areas. There was no law against owning a gun. Still a frontier society, America viewed the ownership and use of a rifle as a matter of survival—even though the frontier was now far removed from the centers of urban activity and about to be subdued forever. In the minds of most Americans, shooting straight was not only the patriotic thing for an individual to do, it was a matter of intense national pride, if not altogether in the national interest.

Perhaps more a matter of national pride than riflery was the sport of boxing. Here, 19th century America could show the world—mostly Great Britain—that it was a robust nation, strong and fearless; that America was not to be taken too lightly, not to be challenged too quickly, lest one wanted to suffer the consequences. Americans felt they could flatten anyone and were always willing to try, or so it seemed. They indulged their free spirit, while demonstrating the manly art of self-defense, by brawling in saloons, clubs, and boxing rings.

Like gouging, a brutal form of wrestling, boxing, or organized fistfighting, was illegal throughout much of America during the 19th century. But unlike gouging, which was never made legal, boxing eventually was legalized in a number of states before the century ended. It took nearly one hundred years for this to happen. It did not take one hundred years for the public to accept the sport, however. With police looking the other way, many a fight between experts took place on a back swamp in New Orleans or on a floating barge in Gravesend Bay, Brooklyn, with a public as interested in the outcome as the promoters.

GOUGING

Again, like a variety of organized sports emerging in America during the 19th century, boxing came from Great Britain and ultimately ancient Greece and Rome, where it all began and where it was finally outlawed. But royal interest in the sport brought it back to life during the 18th century in London, from whence it came to the American colonies.

There were rules—the London Prize Ring Rules—which attempted to keep the fight from degenerating into an eye-gouging, bone-breaking, murderous street-corner brawl. Fighters did not have to wear any gear other than the tight pants they fought in. Moreover they fought bare fisted, or "bare knuckled," until at least 1892, when slugger John L. Sullivan lost the heavyweight championship to James J. Corbett, a scientific gentleman boxer who was not intimidated by Sullivan's 200-pound bulk, his sledgehammer fists, his crude style, or the Irish and American flags he used for a pants belt. The fight took place in New Orleans. The fighters fought under the Marquis of Queensbury Rules for the first time in a championship fight. These rules were established in England in 1865. Fighters had to use gloves—the first time that happened in a championship fight—and fought a set number of three-minute rounds. Among other rules was the ten-count knockdown.

The last bare-knuckled championship fight occurred in 1889 in Mississippi between the very same Sullivan and Jake Kilrain. Sullivan battered Kilrain into submission.

But it took seventy-five rounds to do it. "Why don't you stand up and fight," Sullivan needled Kilrain, as the latter, still on his feet, beaten to a bloody pulp, staggered around the ring near the end of the fight.

Until the Sullivan vs. Corbett fight, no one paid much attention to the Marquis of Queensbury rules, only the London Prize Ring Rules, if any. A fighter could not kick, butt, bite, wrestle, or hit below the belt. Everything else he could think of doing was allowed. A round was decided by a knockdown. Seventy-five knockdowns by one fighter or both equaled seventy-five rounds. Most of these fights went on for hours, with fighters going down like tenpins in a bowling alley. If the fighter was unable to "come to scratch"—to appear at a line drawn across the center of the ring or scratched into the ground—he lost the fight. No one lost just because he was knocked out. He simply could not come to scratch and that was that.

Sometimes one fighter was able to get his opponent into a permissible headlock to prevent him from falling and having a round called, thus giving him a rest and a chance to recover. While in the headlock, the victim would have his head pummeled mercilessly, and then he was allowed to fall unconscious or close to it, unable to recover and come to scratch. Such a beating could go on endlessly, stopped only by the assaulting of the tormentor by the victim's friends. Referees knew better than to interfere. They did not even get into the ring with the fighters once the battle began, preferring to supervise from outside the ropes. None of the rules, however, established weight classes such as heavyweights, middleweights, or lightweights. Small men fought big men. A champ was champ over everyone.

Californian John C. Heenan, an American heavyweight champ in 1860, fought Briton Tom Sayers, a middleweight, in England. Heenan outweighed Sayers by some 40 or 50 pounds. Heenan flattened Sayers 37 times in the two-hour battle, but each time Sayers got up, recovered, and chopped away at Heenan's eyes, nearly blinding him. Surprisingly, Sayers had hurt one of his arms early in the fight and fought some thirty rounds with only one fist. Heenan was unable to beat the smaller man. The fight was a draw.

BARE-FISTED BOXING

Besides the colorful Sullivan, Kilrain, Corbett, and Heenan, America boasted a number of unofficial or illegal champs. One of these was Tom Molineaux, a slave who fought without a loss throughout the South. The huge black man beat every challenger, usually other slaves. He was recognized in 1810 as the best fighter in America and given his freedom. Molineaux went North and then to England, where he lost twice to Tommy Cribbs, the English champion.

"Gentleman Jim" Corbett finally lost his title in 1897 to Bob Fitzsimmons in Carson City, Nevada. Two years later James J. Jeffries beat Fitzsimmons in Coney Island. Jeffries was the last champion of the 19th century, retiring undefeated in 1905.

Mayhem in sports was not confined to the illegal boxing ring, however. College football provided still another arena for the spirited American male, seemingly bent on self-destruction.

Kicking around a leather ball stuffed with sawdust or a wood ball was nothing new in history. The Greeks did it. The Romans copied the Greeks. The medieval Italians did it in a game called calcio. And medieval Englishmen did it. Even American Indians played a game of football that included tackling, blocking, and worse. Everyone got into the game—men, women and children. The game required two teams of at least twelve players each to kick their own ball from one end of a course to another. The first team to reach the goal won. The other team sent players—and sometimes nonplayers—to prevent victory. On Indian courses that often measured anywhere from one to ten miles, ambushes resulting in injuries and sudden death were not uncommon.

The American game of football, however, had its roots in the English game of rugby, first played at Rugby School in Warwickshire, England, in 1823. Unlike soccer, or association football, played at two other English schools, Eton and Harrow, rugby permitted players to carry the ball forward and to tackle the ball carrier.

Students at Yale College in New Haven, Connecticut, had been kicking a ball around for years during the colonial period, much to the annoyance of the college administration. College officials looked upon the activity as ungentlemanly and an affront to morals. But the students persisted. By mid-century, both Yale and Harvard students had developed inter-class rivalries involving the possession of a ball. Groups of freshmen and sophomores, for example, would dare each other to take a ball placed between them. As soon as someone touched the ball, a riot began that left most participants battered and bloodied. This game of "rush" was banned when the Civil War burst upon the nation and college boys went off to fight to the death.

Until Saturday, November 6, 1869, students at one college had never played football with students at another. On that day they did. Rutgers and Princeton played the first intercollegiate football game on record. The game was closer to English-style football (soccer) than to rugby; yet it was neither. The two twenty-five-man teams caught, slapped, and kicked a round ball but never ran with it. The object was to kick it through opposite goal posts. Six points (there was one point per goal kicked) won the game. Rutgers beat Princeton 6-4. Several other games were played over the next couple of years involving Rutgers, Princeton, Yale, and Columbia, but each time the rules were different.

The teams held a meeting in 1872 to establish one set of rules they could all agree to play by. Three years later, after Harvard played McGill University of Canada in a game of rugby-style football, the rules were changed again to establish the intercollegiate game of football to be played fundamentally as it is played today. By 1890 colleges were hiring coaches to field better teams and the game had spread all over the country.

But it remained for one man to invent new techniques and rules that finally changed the look and thrust of the collegiate game to modern football. He was Walter Chauncey Camp, Yale player, captain, coach, and finally Director of Athletics. Camp invented the quarterback position, eleven-man teams, below-waist tackling, and the concept of giving up the football to an opponent if the ball was not advanced a certain number of yards in a given number of plays.

FOOTBALL

For much of the last quarter of the 19th century and on into the 20th century, college football was dominated by eastern schools, chiefly the so-called Ivy League, and within the Ivies by the "Big Three"—Yale, Harvard, and Princeton. These schools fielded such powerhouse teams that they seemed almost invincible over the years. During the 1880's, Yale played a short series against Wesleyan, another Connecticut college. Yale rolled up a grand total of 273 points without ever being scored upon.

The heart of such power, besides the size of the players, was an attacking play called the flying wedge. Here, the ball carrier was hidden in the center of a compact mass of teammates who, holding on to each other, ran at the other team with great speed, hustling the protected ball player along with them.

Death on the football field was not all that frequent, considering the roughness of the game. Injuries abounded in a game that required no substitutions. Football drew blood and large crowds. Before the century had ended, American football had become an established Saturday-afternoon social and athletic event from New York to California.

Another furious game that became popular among college students during the 1880's was lacrosse. The game, which requires teams of twelve players each to kick, throw, or scoop a ball into an opponent's goal with

LACROSSE

a stick having a net at the end, was basically a Canadian game invented by Indians. In fact, North American Indians played the game, or variations of it, well into the 19th century.

The Indian game was simple. One hundred to one thousand warriors divided themselves up into two teams with few rules other than to get a stuffed leather ball through a goal post by any means available, including the use of a stick with a net at one end. The goal-post distances could be anywhere from twice the size of a modern football field—about 200 yards—to 2 miles. The modern game of lacrosse is played on a field about 60 yards wide—it varies—and 110 yards long. The real object of the Indian game, however, was a test of manhood, of endurance, to see which of the players would be the bravest in battle.

French trappers and settlers adopted the game, and it became one of Canada's major national sports. The French Canadians not only gave lacrosse ("the stick") its name, but established the rules by which Americans played the game.

American Indians invented another game using a hook-like stick that eventually developed into various forms of hockey—ice hockey, field hockey, and roller hockey. The only one of these sports to emerge during the 19th century was roller hockey—similar to ice hockey except the players wore roller skates instead of ice skates and played on a polished wood floor instead of on ice. Roller skating itself was a popular pastime during the last decade of the century, but it faded away by 1900.

The Indian hockey game called shinny involved a multitude of participants as in other Indian sports, but on a shorter field, perhaps 300 to 500 yards long. Using sticks similar to modern field hockey sticks, the Indians banged a hard ball back and forth, trying to make goals. Like lacrosse, Indian hockey was an endurance test. Women played the game, too, but less as a test of endurance than as a pastime.

Bowling and bicycling were milder expressions of 19th century sport.

The Dutch brought bowling, or "skittles," to America while the English brought with them a slightly different game of "bowls" that was first played in ancient Rome and is known today as boccie.

The English bowls, or lawn bowling, required no pins. Instead, the bowler rolled a slightly lopsided ball down a grassy alley, aiming toward but trying not to hit a smaller target ball called a jack. The bowler also tried to hit other bowling balls in the way and knock them as far away from the jack as possible. The game faded and was hardly played in America until the 1880s, when it enjoyed a brief revival by the newly formed Dunellen, New Jersey, Bowling Club.

Dutch bowling, on the other hand, was the beginning

of one of the most popular and widespread participant sports in modern America. During most of the 19th century, American bowlers rolled a ball down a polished wood alley at nine pins set up in rows. Heavy gambling swirled around the sport wherever it was played. The Connecticut General Assembly, responding to loud complaints of corruption surrounding the sport of bowling, enacted a law which prohibited nine-pin bowling. It did not take long for bowling enthusiasts to skirt the law and continue bowling legally. They simply added one pin and invented ten-pin bowling, the sport as it is today. To control the sport and reduce its underworld connections, the American Bowling Congress was founded in 1895. The sport was largely organized by men for male bowlers. It was not until 1916 that women organized themselves into the Women's International Bowling Congress.

Bicycling, too, was very popular, both as a sport and as recreation.

The earliest two-wheeled contraption appeared in America about 1800. It was called a walk-along. The driver straddled the machine and propelled it by walking it. There were no gears or pedals. Over the next 50 or 60 years, more mechanical machines were developed in Europe. The first popular bicycle in America was invented by a Frenchman, Pierre Lallement. This bicycle, called a velocipede, or boneshaker, appeared about the end of the Civil War. The driving pedals were connected to the front wheel, which was a good deal larger than the rear wheel. The tires were made of iron fitted over wood rims. Over the next ten years, the front tire grew and the rear tire shrank. Although the "high wheeler" ran more smoothly on new hard-rubber tires, the machine was too difficult to manage. The front wheel was sometimes well over five feet in diameter, making it difficult for short-legged people to gain speed or even reach the pedals from their high perch over it. Besides, the high wheeler fell over most of the time. During the 1880's, tricycles became something of a rage since three wheels seemed to offer more safety.

Also, in the 1880's, women found it impractical to ride a bicycle in their voluminous skirts. Soon a bicycle was designed with a dropped frame to permit ladies to

HIGH WHEELER

VELOCIPEDE (BONESH

BICYCLES

ride in their skirts without having to straddle a crossbar. By 1890, the whole country seemed to be on wheels with air-filled rubber tires. Bicycles built for two or even three riders, called tandems, were a common sight. The last decade of the century—the "Gay Nineties"—was epitomized by more than a million people on bicycles, a sight and pleasure that inspired such memorable songs as:

"Daisy, Daisy, give me your answer, do!
I'm half crazy, all for the love of you!
It won't be a stylish marriage,
I can't afford a carriage,
But you'll look sweet upon the seat
Of a bicycle built for two!"*

TANDEM

---
*Daisy Bell by Harry Dacre, 1892.

The actual sport of cycling may have begun in Massachusetts in 1883 when two men informally raced each other. Before long, oval tracks were built outdoors to accommodate the new fad. By 1891, New York's Madison Square Garden promoted the first six-day bicycle race. But a new machine loomed on the American horizon, the automobile, and soon bicycling would no longer be the craze it had been.

Water sports, other than sailing, were practically nonexistent during the 19th century. While the well-to-do held their regattas and formed yacht clubs—the most illustrious being the New York Yacht Club, founded by the same John Stevens who owned Hoboken's Elysian Fields—others, too, enjoyed racing their small boats everywhere. America was a maritime nation and before long would demonstrate that she, not England, ruled the ocean deep.

In 1850, Britain's Royal Yacht Club invited Stevens—now Commodore Stevens—to participate in a race with British boats around the Isle of Wight. Stevens built a special racing schooner for the occasion and christened her *America*. A year later, the 101 foot 9 inch raked-masted boat took on sixteen of England's fastest racing yachts and beat them all. The Americans were awarded a silver cup dubbed the America's Cup, took it home with them, and bolted it to a table in the New York Yacht Club. More than 125 years later, America still had not lost the cup.

AMERICA

The racing of small, oared boats was largely confined to American colleges. Until 1857, college crews raced on rivers, using slow and clumsy boats. But in 1857, Harvard put seven men—six oarsmen and a steerer-leader, called a coxwain—into a fragile, slender, lightweight "shell" and beat the competition handily. By 1870, most eastern colleges were manning six-oared shells and racing each other by a set of rules formalized by the Rowing Association of American Colleges. This was not the first such association in America, however. That honor belonged to New York's Castle Garden Amateur Boat Club, founded in 1834.

CREW

In 1875, thirteen eastern colleges* put their six-oared shells into New York's Lake Saratoga and staged a mammoth race. Cornell won. But Yale and Harvard, who had been racing each other since 1852, complained about mismanagement and the hazards of a shell-crowded three-mile course. They withdrew from the association, preferring to race each other only.

From time to time, single oared "sculling" captured the public imagination, but it remained for the bigger boats to maintain a wider interest in oared boat racing.

*Amherst, Bowdoin, Columbia, Cornell, Dartmouth, Hamilton, Harvard, Princeton, Trinity, Union, Wesleyan, Williams, and Yale.

Although America boasted a number of speedy professional runners between 1830 and 1870—sprinters like George Steward, who ran 100 yards in about 10 seconds (1847); and distance runner William Jackson, who loped along a 10-mile course in just under an hour—it was not until the Civil War had ended that running for money gave way to pure sport in the tradition of classical Greece—amateur track and field. The amateur concept in America was begun by the newly founded New York Athletic Club. Eight years later, those same eastern schools which were rowing and playing football were holding track and field meets under the auspices of another new organization, the Intercollegiate Association of Amateur Athletes in

AN OLYMPIC RACE

America—the IC4A. These meets included varied-distance foot racing as well as hurdles, discus and javelin throwing, shot-put, jumping, and the like. In 1888, the new AAU—the Amateur Athletic Union—began supervising all American amateur athletics, collegiate and non-collegiate.

In 1896, a handful of American college athletes went to Athens, Greece, to participate in the first Olympic Games to be held since the end of the fourth century A.D., when Roman Emperor Theodosius banned them. By that time, Greece had become a conquered province of Rome and the games had become corrupt. Women were permitted to attend the games for the first time in 1896, but it was not until 1912, when the Olympics were held in

Stockholm, Sweden, that they were allowed to compete.

In 1896, after about 1,500 years, a few athletes representing eight nations pitted their athletic skills against one another. Thirteen events appeared on the schedule and the United States athletes won nine of them.*

The 19th century passed into history on the legs, so to speak, of a fast moving 20th century ball game—basketball—created during its last decade by a college gym instructor.

Dr. James Naismith, who taught physical education at the Young Men's Christian Association International Training School—later chartered as Springfield College in Massachusetts—was asked by the school's athletic director, Dr. Luther Gulick, to invent an indoors game to keep some of the restless athletes busy during the winter months. Naismith responded after some thought by nailing two peach baskets to balcony rails at each end of the college gym. He divided the eighteen men in his class into two teams. He gave them a soccer ball and explained a few basic rules he had dreamed up which required them to aim at the other team's basket and score points by arcing the ball into the basket. That was in 1891. He also had to station a student on a ladder at each

---

*100- and 400- meter runs: Thomas Burke (USA); 800- and 1500- meter runs: Thomas Flack (England); Marathon: Spyros Loues (Greece); 110-meter hurdles: Thomas Curtis (U.S.A.); long jump and running high jump: Ellery Clark (U.S.A.); triple jump: James Connolly (U.S.A.); pole vault: William Hoyt (U.S.A.); discus and 16-pound shot-put: Robert Garrett (U.S.A.); 100-meter freestyle swimming: Alfred Hajos (Hungary).

BASKETBALL

end of the court to retrieve the ball from the basket. It was not until later that the bottoms of the baskets were removed to allow the ball to drop through for quicker recovery, adding to the speed of the game which was called by the school newspaper the following year, "The New Game."

In 1893, women students at Smith College nearby began playing the new game. In that same year the first intercollegiate basketball game was played: the University of Iowa vs. Geneva College in Pennsylvania. Within three years, most sports-minded New England colleges were playing basketball in their indoor gyms, provided they had one. Finally, Dr. Naismith's nine-man team was reduced to five-man teams, in 1897, and modern basketball was born.

Of all the organized, competitive sports to come alive in America during the 19th century, basketball seemed to epitomize the restless, inventive, and free-spirited American character. The game came at the end of one era and the beginning of another, straddling an American sporting world that reflected a hustling and self-confident society.

Index

796
Fis

Fisher, Leonard Everett
The Sports

81-602

DATE DUE	BORROWER'S NAME	
10-9-85	Ryan	

81-602

796
Fis

Fisher, Leonard Everett
The Sports